THE 5,000 FRIENDS

OF VERONICA VEETCH

Written by Jean Hanson | Illustrated by Launie Parry

BAILIWICK PRESS

*For my sister, Barbara, who shares her love of books
with her kindergarten students.*

*Thanks to: Launie Parry, whose illustrations are worth more
than my thousand words; Slow Sand Writers Society; and most of all,
editor extraordinaire Karla Oceanak, who contributed
more to this book than I care to admit.*

— J.H.

For my family, who means the world to me.

*Thanks to Jean for writing the words that inspired me.
And to Karla and Kendra for believing in me and keeping me on track!*

— L.P.

PUBLISHED BY: Bailiwick Press | 309 East Mulberry Street, Fort Collins, Colorado 80524
www.bailiwickpress.com

MANUFACTURED BY: Friesens Corporation | Altona, Canada | July 2017 | Job # 233992

BOOK DESIGN BY: Launie Parry | Red Letter Creative | www.red-letter-creative.com

ISBN 978-1-934649-27-5

PRINTED IN CANADA

27   26   24   23   22   21   20   19   18   17   10   9   8   7   6   5   4   3   2   1

Veronica Veetch was a curious girl,
from the size of her teeth to the swirl of her curl—
a ringlet that coiled from the tip of her chin
then wound its way down to the top of her shin.

Veronica Veetch talked
of many fine things,
like operas and oysters and
gleaming gold rings.

She knew how to curtsy,
tie bowties, and fence.
The words she liked best
were extremely immense.

To show you a samba or swift minuet,
she'd whirl through the room
without breaking a sweat.

If you needed a no-nonsense
nautical knot,
she'd twist that up too,
as if reared on a yacht.

Then wearing a boa, she'd bid you adieu.
"I'm off to Samoa, Tibet, and Peru!"

For someone their own age,
the other kids thought,
this Veronica Veetch knew an awfully lot.

According to one boy, the big bossy Bob,
Veronica lived like a richy-rich snob.

"How else would she know all that fancy-pants stuff?"
he grumbled and griped in a hotheaded huff.

"Her family has servants! And art in gold frames!
They gobble up fish eggs and watch polo games!"

Did the children believe him?
You bet your patootie.
They now were convinced
that this Veetch girl was snooty.

It made the kids cranky
and Millicent mad.
"Veronica has things
that *I've* never had."

"I told you," sneered Bob.
"She's too big for her britches.
As if we should care
about all of her riches."

"Oh yes," Nikki nodded.
"I tend to agree.
She's putting on airs
that smell stinky to me."

Said Curt with a crew cut,
"And what's with her hair?"

Then Dante decided,
"It just isn't fair!"

And so they agreed it was high time to teach
a lesson, much-needed, to Veronica Veetch.

Beginning that moment, the kids stayed away.
Not one of her classmates asked V.V. to play.

And when she approached them?
I bet you can guess.
They turned on their heels.
Downright mean, I confess!

But Veronica didn't act lonely or bored. Nor did she fuss about being ignored.

She wrote in her best script—and sent, in the mail—
an offer so charming it just couldn't fail:

Oh please won't you join me on Sunday at 3
for tiramisu and a smidgen of tea?

If you'll come to my house for a nibble and sip,
I'll gleefully give you a round-the-world trip.

The invite was lavish—quite tempting indeed.
The kids asked permission; their parents agreed.

They gabbled and gossiped their way across town,
yet once they reached V.V.'s, they quieted down.

The house was in shambles, ramshackle and small.
It seemed that the shutters and chimney might fall.
The roof on the right sank alarmingly low,
and the grass in the yard was in need of a mow.

Befuddled and baffled,
they eyed the address.
Perhaps they were wrong,
but they knocked nonetheless.

Out peeked the curl
and the baby-tooth grin.
"Oh goody, you're here!
Won't you kindly come in?"

When she stepped to the side,
swinging open the door...

...they saw
hundreds
of books,
stacked
from
ceiling
to floor.

They were ordered by subject,
from *A*s down to *Z*s,
and Veronica said,
"They're arranged for my ease.
With this many books,
my approach is precise.
Misplacing the *M*s would
mean missing the mice."

"The hallway is home
to the Hobbits and hares,
and a curious chimp is
chucked under those chairs."

"In my bed beneath blankets
I bunk with a bat.
And on top of my covers?
A top-hatted cat."

"If it's piglets or princes
that you'd like to meet,
they're perched on the porch
with a plum parakeet."

"I had quite the quandary
corraling Australia—
a country that comes
with such odd paraphernalia.

But since its marsupial
starts with a *K*, the kitchen
was perfect to file it away.

The cockatoos, emus,
and didgeridoos
are stacked on the counter
above kangaroos.

And now for the fun.
Where would *you* like to go?
Anywhere you imagine
would be apropos."

Though Nikki was picky,
she soon started chuckling,
then wandered through Boston
in search of a duckling.

A bullfight in Spain
had Bob shouting "Olé!"
The best bull of all
calmly sniffed a bouquet.

Millicent journeyed
to Paris, in France,
and bunked with twelve girls
in a vine-covered manse.

An atlas of Chile
gave Curtis a grin.
A place so delicious
was terribly thin!

Dante read novels
and went, we presume,
the farthest of all
without leaving the room.

The children were having magnificent fun
and began to feel sorry for what they had done.

"We envied so wrongly your limos and jewels,
safaris and mansions
and huge swimming pools…"

"I quite understand.
 In a way you were right,"
 said Veronica Veetch,
 who was always polite.

"One look at my books
 and you can't help but see,
 I *do* have great riches
 heaped high around me.

I don't read my books
 just for homework or study—
 they're my playmates, my pals,
 my companions, my buddies.

If you add them all up,
 from the kitchen to bath—
 that's 5,000 friends.
 Go ahead…do the math!"

"And how about this?
I'll send each of you back
with as many new friends as
you're able to stack."

The children said thank you
and to their own homes
carried novels and histories
and oodles of poems.

And the brainy book lover who started this tale?
While reading one Sunday, her color turned pale.

As she came to the page with the book's final word,
she slowly slowed down, till her pace was absurd.

She'd finished a guide to the zyzzyva weevil,
a wretched big bug, rather ugly and evil.

No wonder Veronica felt so bereft!
She was done with the Zs, and now no books were left.

But just as fat tears filled Veronica's eyes,
her friends arrived saying, "We've got a surprise!
There's truly no reason to be so distressed.
This world contains more books than you've ever guessed.

Let's check them out now. It's not at all hard...

...we'll just go and get you a library card!"

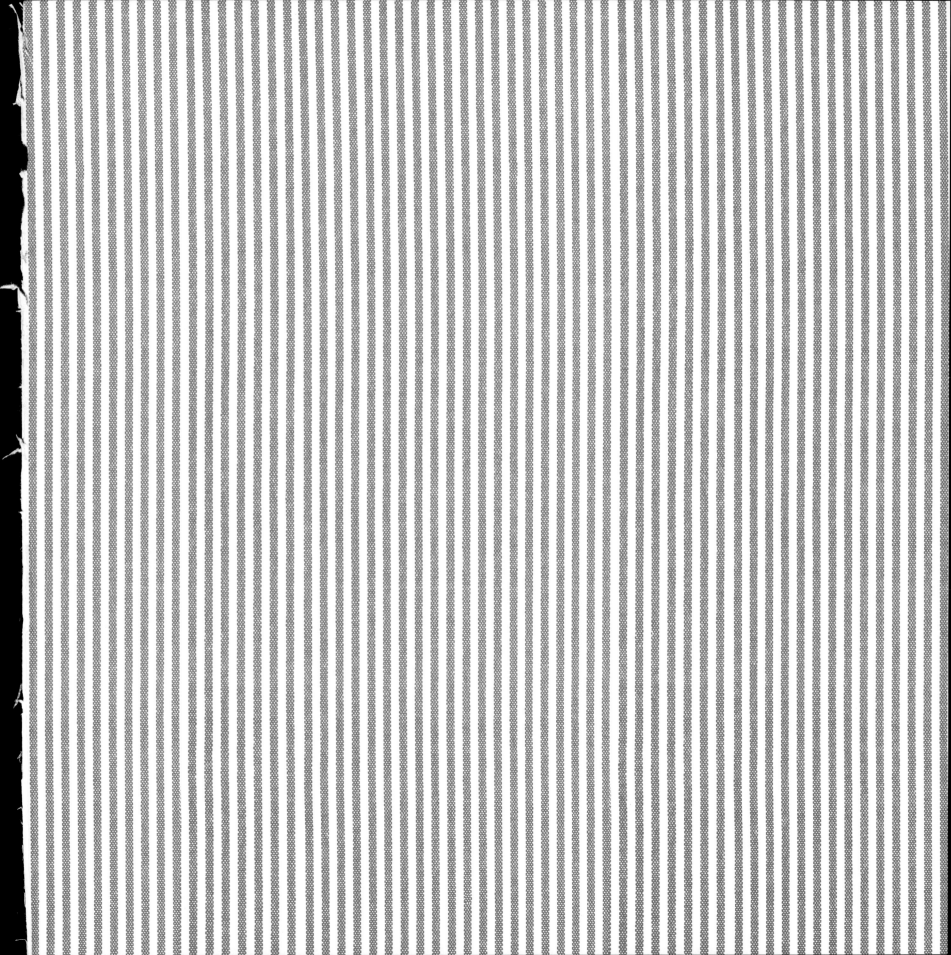